A.J.'s Rules
for School

Dan Gutman

Pictures by
Jim Paillot

HARPER
An Imprint of HarperCollinsPublishers

My Weird School: A.J.'s Rules for School

Text copyright © 2018 by Dan Gutman

Illustrations copyright © 2018 by Jim Paillot

www.harpercollinschildrens.com

Typography by Laura Mock

❖

First Edition

No More
Mr. Nice Guy

 My name is A.J. and I hate rules.
Rules aren't cool. Rules are cruel. Rules are for fools.

 I disagree! My name is Andrea and I *love* rules! Rules tell us what we're supposed to do! If it weren't for rules, Arlo, how would we know how to behave?

 Oh no! It's Andrea Young, that annoying girl in my class with

1

curly brown hair! She calls me by my real name because she knows I don't like it. Who let *you* in here, Andrea?

 Arlo, you know perfectly well why I'm here. We're supposed to write this *together* as a group project for the gifted and talented program.

 Shhhh! Don't tell everybody I'm in the gifted and talented pro-gram! They'll think I'm a nerd like you.*

 I am *not* a nerd, Arlo!

 You are too!

 R2D2!

---

* What are you looking down here for? The story is up *there*!

Andrea and I went back and forth like that for a while. But then the weirdest thing in the history of the world happened. An announcement came over the loudspeaker.

Well, that's not the weird part, because announcements come over the loudspeaker all the time. The weird part was what happened after *that*.

It was Mrs. Patty, the school secretary. She announced, "All classes please report to the all-purpose room for an assembly."

I don't know why they call it "the all-purpose room." You can't use it for *all* purposes. I mean, you can't go horseback riding in there.

When we got to the all-purpose room, our principal, Mr. Klutz, was up on the stage.

 He has no hair at all. I mean *none*.

 Mr. Klutz was with Miss Lazar, the school custodian. They were both soaking wet. Mr. Klutz looked like he was in a bad mood.

 And Miss Lazar was holding a toilet bowl plunger in her hand.

 Oh yeah. And everybody was talking, as usual. Not *me*, of course. We're supposed to be quiet during assemblies. Mr. Klutz made a peace sign with his fingers.

 That means "shut up."

Everybody stopped talking. Mr. Klutz said he was really disappointed with us. Some of the kids—not *me*, of course—have been breaking the rules at Ella Mentry School. He said, "From now on, the rules of the school are going to be strictly enforced."

 Mr. Klutz was *really* mad. He said, "Things are going to change around here, starting right now. No more Mr. Nice Guy."

 Then he pulled out this big scroll and started reading a list of new rules for school. The first one was NO RUNNING IN THE HALLWAY.

 Well, I guess that makes sense. When you run in the hallway, you could crash into somebody. Kids could get hurt.

The second one was NO CHEWING GUM IN SCHOOL.

 I can live with that. It's kind of gross when you find old, chewed-up gum stuck all over the place.

 The next one was NO BASEBALL CAPS.

 I don't understand that one. Who cares what's on top of my head? Am I going to learn better if I'm not wearing a baseball cap?

 The list went on and on. NO CONGREGATING IN THE HALLWAYS. NO UNTIED SHOES.

 NO LOUD VOICES. NO PULLING HAIR.

 NO CLIMBING THE FENCE. NO PLAYING KEEP AWAY.

NO WALKING ON THE GRASS.
NO TOYS IN SCHOOL.

 NO PENS WITH RED INK. NO
BACKPACKS WITH WHEELS. NO
JUMPING UP AND DOWN. NO WALKING
BACKWARD. NO SHORT SHORTS. NO
JOKES. NO CUPCAKES FOR BIRTHDAY
PARTIES....

 WHAT?! By that point, we were all
freaking out. No cupcakes? Was
he kidding me? *Everybody* brings cupcakes
for birthday parties. That's the first rule of
being a kid!

 I think Mr. Klutz was going overboard with all those new rules.

 He fell out of a boat? I didn't
see any boats in the all-purpose
room.

7

No, Arlo, I mean Mr. Klutz was getting carried away with all those new rules.

 I didn't see anybody carry him away. I would have noticed *that*.

 No, dumbhead! You know what I mean! Even the teachers looked shocked. A bunch of them were whispering to each other in the back of the room.

 Mr. Klutz's new rules were getting weirder and weirder. Finally, he got to the last rule on his list. It was the weirdest rule of all. But I'm not going to tell you what it was.

Okay, okay, I'll tell you. But you have to read the next chapter, so nah-nah-nah boo-boo on you.

The Last Rule

Mr. Klutz read off the last rule on his list—NO FLUSHING TOYS DOWN THE TOILET. Miss Lazar held up a doll, which she obviously fished out of the toilet bowl. That's when everybody looked at Arlo. I can't believe you flushed a doll down the toilet!

It's not a doll! It's an *action figure*. His name is Striker Smith, and he's a cool superhero who fights crime. He's my favorite toy.

 And what was he doing in the toilet bowl, Arlo?

 Well, I was in the boys' bathroom with my friends Ryan, Michael, and Neil. We were acting out this famous scene where Striker Smith chases some bad guys around a water park. We were dangling Striker over the bowl. That's when

somebody leaned on that handle thingy you use to flush the toilet. And uh, well... let's just say Striker Smith met his watery end. But it was an accident!

Arlo, that is just about the dumbest thing you have *ever* done! And you've done a lot of dumb things. Why didn't you fish your toy out of the bowl?

 Are you crazy? I'm not going to stick my hand into a toilet bowl! I didn't know what to do. I didn't know what to say. I had to think fast!

 So your solution was to just run out of the boys' room?

 Yes! When you do something really dumb, you're supposed to get out of there fast, before anybody finds out. That's the first rule of being a kid. Didn't you ever flush something down a toilet by accident?

 No! *Nobody* does that! I play with my dolls in a *nice* way. I dress them up and have them go to parties, and—

11

Ugh. I think I'm gonna throw up. Anyway, Mr. Klutz is usually nice, but this time he was *really* mad. And he was really wet too, because he and Miss Lazar had to take apart the toilet bowl after it overflowed.

 Usually at the end of an assembly, Mr. Klutz brings in some grown-up who we never met before. But not this time. He just yelled "Dismissed!" and told us to go to our first period class. He was really upset. It was all your fault, Arlo.

So is your face.*

---

* If somebody says something mean to you and you can't think of a good comeback, just say "So is your face." That's the first rule of being a kid.

Mrs. Roopy Is Loopy

 Our first period class was library, so we had to walk a million hundred miles down the hallway. I hate library.

 Our librarian is named Mrs. Roopy. But today she looked funny. She had a beard, for one thing. She was wearing overalls and she was carrying a shovel in one hand.

And she had a pot on her head. That was strange. So I asked her, "Mrs. Roopy, why do you have a pot on your head?"

 "Who's Roopy?" said Mrs. Roopy. "You young 'uns must be confusin' me with some other feller. Johnny

Appleseed's the name. Plantin' apple trees is my game."

 Oh yeah. Mrs. Roopy doesn't like to admit that she's our librarian. You never know who she's going to be from one day to the next. Sometimes she dresses up like George Washington. Or Neil Armstrong. Or Little Bo Peep. She's weird.

 I asked Mrs. Roopy—I mean Johnny Appleseed—if she was going to read us a story.

 She said, "Nah, I reckon I'm gonna travel from town to town plantin' apple trees most everywhere I wander. You young 'uns wanna join me?"

"Why, are you coming apart?" I asked.

 I told Mrs. Roopy we're not allowed to leave school grounds in the middle of the day. That's a rule. Then I asked her if we could check out books from the library. She replied, "Nope. I reckon that ain't allowed no more."

 WHAT?! It's a *library*! It's filled with *books*. And we weren't allowed to check them out? That was weird.

 "Why not?" I asked her. She replied, "Because that's the rule!"

 It's not fair! Mrs. Roopy is loopy!

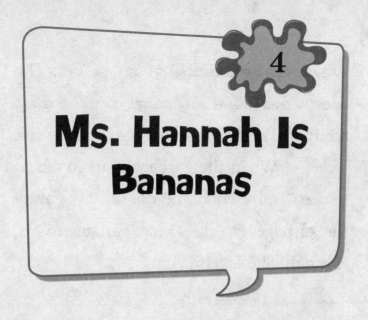

Ms. Hannah Is Bananas

After library, it was time for art. I hate art. We walked a million hundred miles to the art room. It was like walking across the Grand Canyon, so we all stopped to drink from the water fountain on the way.

So we got to the art room, and our art teacher, Ms. Hannah, was wearing a pretty dress that she made out of old potholders. You see, she never throws anything

17

away, because *everything* can be art. She doesn't even have a garbage can in the art room! So there's junk all over the place in there.

 When the garbage man comes to our school, he doesn't take away the garbage. He gives *more* garbage to Ms. Hannah! She's weird.

 I asked Ms. Hannah, "Are we going to draw pictures today? I love drawing pictures!"

 She said no.

 I asked, "Are we going to finger paint?"

 She said no again.

I asked, "Are we going to make sculptures out of clay?" She said no *again*! She told us, "Today we're going to create artwork using our imaginations. We're going to use our brains."

 WHAT?! If you only make art in your brain, how can you stick it to the refrigerator when you get home? I asked Ms. Hannah, "Can we use some art supplies?" She said no again.*

 Everybody was asking "Why not?" And Ms. Hannah replied, "Because that's the new rule. No more art supplies."

It's not fair! Ms. Hannah is bananas!

---

* Are you enjoying the book so far? Do you need a pillow? We want you to be comfortable.

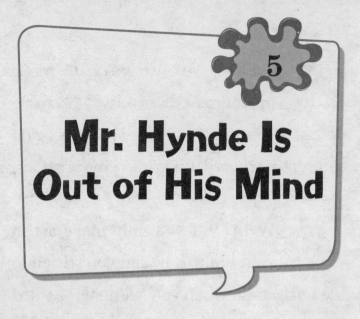

5

Mr. Hynde Is Out of His Mind

It was weird to sit around making art in my head. I was glad when it was finally over. But then it was time for music. I hate music. We walked a million hundred miles to the music room.

I love music! My favorite play is *Annie*. Would you like to hear me sing "Tomorrow," Arlo?

As long as you don't sing "Today," I'll be happy. Actually, I'd really like you to sing "Never."

 Very funny.

 Our music teacher is Mr. Hynde. He's a rapper who was on that TV show *American Idol*. Rapping is cool. It's just like regular music, except for the music part. One time, Mr. Hynde banged his hands on Mr. Klutz's head like it was a bongo drum. He's weird.

 There are all kinds of interesting instruments in the music room—drums, keyboards, pianos, recorders...

 Hey, how come it's called a recorder if it doesn't record anything? That doesn't make any sense at all.

 Maybe it was invented by somebody named Miss Recorder. Anyway, when we got to the music room, Mr. Hynde told us that the greatest musical instrument of all is the human brain.

So naturally I asked him if we could play bongos on each other's heads. He said, "No. From now on, we're going to play music *in* our heads." WHAT?!

 I said, "You mean we can't play with any of the instruments?" Mr. Hynde said no.

 "Can't I at least beat on a drum?" I asked. He said no.

 We all asked, "Why not?" and Mr. Hynde replied, "Because that's the new rule!"

 It's not fair! Mr. Hynde is out of his mind!

Miss Small Is off The Wall

 Playing music in my head was boring. I was glad when it was finally over. Then we had to go to fizz ed. I hate fizz ed. Instead of playing football or something cool, we always have to do weird stuff like juggle scarves or balance feathers on one finger. We walked a million hundred miles to the gym.

 Our gym teacher is Miss Small. She's really tall. One time we were playing a game called Ghost in the Graveyard and she fell out of a tree and broke her arm. That was scary!

After all that time sitting around doing nothing in library, art, and music, I was excited to go to fizz ed and get some exercise. I didn't care *what* exercise we did, as long as it wasn't sitting around doing nothing.

I asked Miss Small, "Are we going to balance feathers on our fingers today?" She said no. "Are we going to juggle scarves?" I asked. She said no.

Miss Small told us that instead of doing that stuff, we were going to do something called "meditation." I didn't know what that meant, but it didn't sound like fun.

She told us that meditation is *mental* exercise. She had us all sit on the floor and told us to stay quiet and focus on our breathing. She said, "Breathe in. Breathe out. Now breathe in again."

 WHAT?! I was *already* breathing in and out before we got to fizz ed! I've been breathing in and out my whole life. In fact, if I *didn't* breathe in and out for just a few minutes, I'd be dead! If you ask me, this meditation thing was a lot like sitting around and doing nothing.

 After a few minutes of meditation, I was getting bored. I asked Miss Small, "Can we go outside and run around the playground or something now?" She said no.

 We all shouted, "Why not?" and Miss Small said, "Because that's the new rule!"

It's not fair! Miss Small is off the wall!

Forbidden Fruit

 It seemed like *all* the teachers at Ella Mentry School had gone *crazy*!

 After fizz ed, we walked a million hundred miles to the vomitorium to eat lunch.* We all had peanut butter and jelly sandwiches, except for Ryan. He had a

---

* It used to be called the cafetorium, but then some first grader threw up in there.

jelly and peanut butter sandwich.

 "The teachers are weirder than *ever* today," said Michael. "They won't let us do *anything*."

 "Yeah, this place is turning into a jail," I said. "They might as well put us in cells."

I don't know why you were complaining, Arlo. You always say you hate library, music, art, and gym anyway.

I *do* hate all that stuff. But when somebody tells me I can't do something, it makes me want to do it!

 Ah, forbidden fruit.

 Huh? What does fruit have to do with anything? I'm eating a peanut butter and jelly sandwich. I hate fruit.

 Forget it, Arlo.

 Anyway, we had a long talk about whether or not Ella Mentry School was turning into a jail. That's when I came up with the greatest idea in the history of the world. I told the gang, "Maybe these people aren't our real teachers. Did you ever think of that?"

I asked Arlo, "What do you mean?"

 "Well," I told her, "maybe we're living in a parallel universe where teachers pretend to be real teachers but they're really evil robotic teacher clones."

 I told Arlo to stop trying to scare Emily.

 Emily said, "I'm scared." Then Ryan said, "Maybe the evil robotic teacher clones are trying take over the world!" That's when Emily yelled, "We've got to *do* something!" And then she went running out of the vomitorium. Emily is weird.

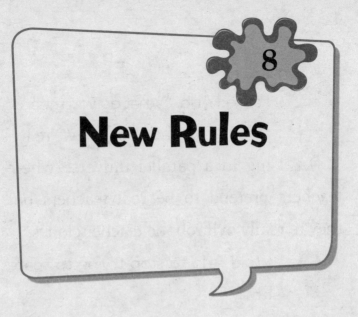

New Rules

 But Emily was right, for once in her life. We *did* have to do something. But what?

 I think it was Ryan who suggested we make up a list of our *own* rules and give them to Mr. Klutz.

 Yeah, Ryan should get the Nobel Prize for *that* idea.*

---

* That's a prize they give out to people who don't have bells.

I always carry a pad and pencil with me in case I need to write something down. So we started making a list of Rules for School.

 Everybody started shouting out ideas—No more homework! Free ice cream sundaes at lunch! All day recess! No more report cards! Every day is Pizza Day! Snow days even when it isn't snowing outside! Pin the tail on the teacher!

 Personally, I didn't think those ideas were so great. There was no way that Mr. Klutz was going to agree to all those rules. But maybe he would agree to some of them.

 I said we should demand to have new desks with video games built into them. You know, like when you're on an airplane and they have a screen in the seatback in front of you? Those things are cool. We should have them built right into our desks so if the teacher gets boring, we could just play video games instead of paying attention.

 That's crazy, Arlo. Mr. Klutz would never agree to that.

 Hey, they said Thomas Edison was crazy, but he invented the light bulb, right? If he hadn't invented the light bulb, we would never have any ideas, because whenever you have an idea, a light bulb appears over your head.

 Instead of going to recess, we took our list of rules and went to Mr. Klutz's office. And do you know what he was doing in there? He was hanging upside down

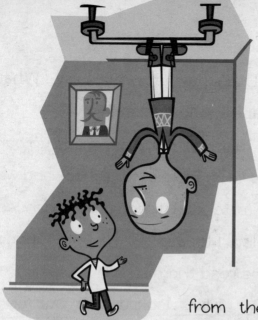

from the ceiling!

Mr. Klutz has these special boots that attach to a pole so he can hang upside down. He says when the blood rushes to his head, it helps him think.

 He also has a punching bag and a foosball table in his office. Mr. Klutz is nuts!

When we walked in the doorway, Mr. Klutz said, "To what do I owe the pleasure of your company?"

That's how grown-ups say, "What are *you* doing here?"

 We told him that we made up our own list of rules for school, and we wanted him to look them over. I handed him the list. He was still hanging upside down as he read them.

 Mr. Klutz looked over our new rules for a million hundred minutes. Then he gave them back to Andrea and said, "I'm sorry, kids, but these rules are just silly. This is a *school*. It's a place for learning, not a place for eating ice cream and playing video games."

 I *knew* we shouldn't have given Mr. Klutz all those crazy rules!

 Bummer in the summer! I thought that was the end of it. But you'll never believe who walked into the door at that moment.

Nobody! It would hurt if you walked into a door. Doors are made of wood. Any dumbhead knows that. But you'll never believe who walked into the door*way*.

 It was Mrs. Roopy, Ms. Hannah, Mr. Hynde, and Miss Small! Suddenly, it was really crowded in Mr. Klutz's office.

 "To what do I owe the pleasure of your company?" asked Mr. Klutz.

 The teachers said they didn't like his new rules, so they made up their own list of Rules for School.

 "Not you too!" said Mr. Klutz.

 Mrs. Roopy handed the list to Mr. Klutz. He was still hanging upside down from the ceiling. He looked over the list very carefully. We couldn't see what it said on the teachers' list of rules. Mr. Klutz didn't say anything.

 We were all on pins and needles.

Well, not really. We were just standing there. If we were on pins and needles, it would have hurt. But there was electricity in the air.

Well, not exactly. If there was electricity in the air, we all would have been electrocuted. But it was really exciting!

 Finally, Mr. Klutz pulled his feet out of his boots and hopped down off the ceiling. "You're right," he said. "I guess I went overboard with all those rules."

 What?! Why is everybody always talking about boats?

Nobody was talking about boats, Arlo! Mr. Klutz was saying that his new rules went too far. He said we could forget about all the silly rules he had given us. We could go back to being a normal school again. Well, as normal as our weird school would *ever* be.

 Everybody started yelling and screaming and shrieking and hooting and hollering and freaking out.

 We were all really happy.

 While the kids were leaving, I sneaked over to Mr. Klutz's desk to get a peek at the teachers' list of rules. And you'll never believe what it said on their list.

I'm not going to tell you.

Okay, okay, I'll tell you. It said this, over and over and over again:

BE A NICE PERSON.

 Well, that's pretty much what happened. Sometimes rules can be bad, and sometimes rules can be good. I guess it depends on who's making the rules.

 That's true. I've been giving this a lot of thought. Do you know who should make up all the rules?

 Who?

 Me! So that's why I made up a list of my *own* rules. Everything on the list is number one because they're all. . .

The First Rule of Being a Kid

By A.J.

❀ If you want to get something from a grown-up, say "please" over and over again until they can't stand it anymore. The more times you say "please," the better chance they'll say "yes."

❀ If you don't want to get called on, don't make eye contact with the teacher. By law, they can't call on you if you're looking at your feet.

❀ Parents should never come into your class, unless it's your birthday and they bring cupcakes.

🌸 Always laugh at the principal's jokes, no matter how lame they are.

🌸 If somebody tells you that you did something dumb, act like you did it on purpose.

🌸 When a grown-up tells you a boring story about when they were a kid, always pretend to be interested.

🌸 Green is a weird color. Don't ever eat stuff that's green.

🌸 If you do something really dumb and you don't want to get blamed, start whistling. Because if you're whistling, nobody thinks you did anything wrong.

🌸 When you're in a car with your parents, always ask if you're there yet even though you know perfectly well that you're not there yet.

✸ If you get called down to the principal's office, walk as slowly as you possibly can. The slower you walk, the longer it takes to get anywhere. If you walk slowly enough, by the time you get to the principal's office, he might forget the bad thing that you did.

✸ Any time your parents ask what you did at school during the day, always say "nothin'." Even if an alien spaceship landed in the middle of the lunchroom, just tell your mom that nothing happened.

✸ If you can make a grown-up rub their forehead with their fingers, they'll agree to just about anything.

✸ If you make a joke and nobody laughs, pretend that you never made the joke and keep talking.

* When your mom or dad comes into your classroom, you should always hide under your desk.

* If you ever want something really badly, look at your parents with puppy-dog eyes.

* If a grown-up is about to say something you don't want to hear, change the subject as soon as possible.

* You know a joke is good if you can make milk come out of somebody's nose.*

---

* I guess you're pretty proud of yourself for finishing this book. Well, that's one My Weird School book down, and sixty-five to go!

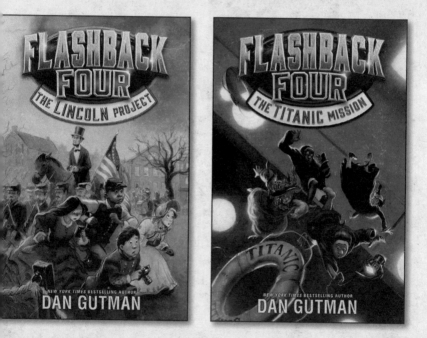